I0764786

The Ghosts Among Us

Darke, Preble & Randolph Counties

Also by Rita Arnold

Ghosts of Darke County
Ghosts of Darke County II
Ghosts of Darke County III
Ghosts of Darke County IV

The Ghosts Among Us

Darke, Preble & Randolph Counties

By
Rita Arnold

White Dog Books

ISBN# 0-9788463-9-7
Library of Congress Catalogue

Cover Design by Ron D'Allessandris

Printed in the United States of America

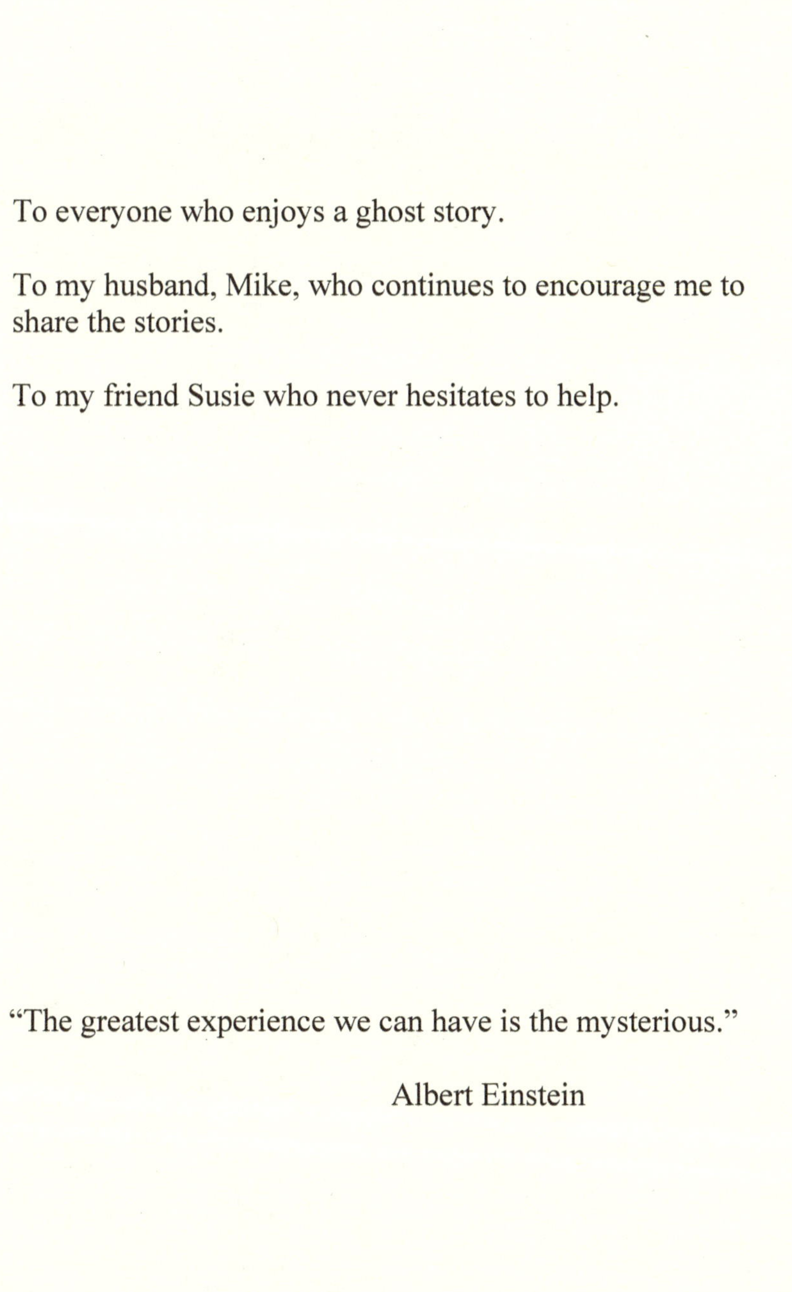

To everyone who enjoys a ghost story.

To my husband, Mike, who continues to encourage me to share the stories.

To my friend Susie who never hesitates to help.

"The greatest experience we can have is the mysterious."

Albert Einstein

People have often wondered,
To themselves and even aloud,
Do ghosts really live here on earth?
Or just float around on a cloud?

This question has always puzzled,
The young and especially the old,
So we're going to settled the question,
By a method that is Oh so bold.

Inside we have gathered some stories,
And we've put them side by side,
We invite you now to read them,
And then we'll let YOU decide!

Milton Arnold

Table of Contents

Darke County Stories

1. The Broken Heart

This story was shared with me several years ago by a man born and raised in Hillgrove, Ohio located northwest of Greenville. He and I met accidentally at a Dayton hospital where I was employed and he was a patient who returned for frequent medical treatments over the years. We shared many enjoyable hours visiting and sharing memories of our mutual home county. In fact, we soon discovered that we were very distantly related. We were both descendents of a pioneer family that arrived in Darke County around 1800.

When I met Richard I was working in Dayton, Ohio and was thrilled to meet someone who grew up just west of Hillgrove, a small rural farming area. We would compare names of people we knew, talk about various past events, the local hang outs that we both enjoyed while growing up (or the lack of hang outs), and had great fun discovering who and what we had in common. In spite of our age difference, Richard was in his late 60's and I was in my mid 30's, we both enjoyed sharing memories of our youths and telling tales of our various adventures. I believe that some of the tales got better with the passing of the years resulting in the embellishment of them.

Some of my co-workers would encourage us to share our stories about our homeland, including the sad, the funny, and of course the ghost stories.

Richard was born and raised southwest of Hillgrove in the early 1930's. He lived on the family farm with his three brothers and two sisters. His cousins, aunts, and uncles all lived on various neighboring farms, all helping each other when needed with their farm work. All Richard ever wanted out of life was to be a farmer; he thought this was the perfect life, working out of doors, being his own boss, and doing what he loved.

Unfortunately World War II broke out and soon Richard was drafted into the army. Richard was sad about leaving his family and the farm but at the same time he was excited about fighting for his country. After months of Army training Richard was sent to a base in New Jersey from which he would be shipped overseas.

While awaiting departure Richard met and married within a week's time a beautiful young lady from New York City. After a very short two days of married life, sadly the time came for Richard to board the troop ship for transport to Europe. Richard fought with the infantry throughout the war, survived the battles and returned uninjured to his wife to truly start their married life together. Before Richard left for Europe he and his wife never discussed plans for life after the war; after all they were young, in love, and on their honeymoon.

Well, she made it very clear that she would never live in the country or even a small town. Richard, being in love, agreed to live in a city. Soon the couple moved to Ohio and Richard went to work in a factory in Dayton. Even though they lived only an hour away from Richard's boyhood home farm, they rarely came to Darke County for a visit. His family would make the trip to Richard's house for occasional visits but Richard's wife had no desire to visit the family farm.

Richard loved his wife and wanted her to be happy, so sadly he complied with her wishes.

Throughout Richard's married life there would be times when he had private thoughts about his childhood adventures on the farm. He learned to keep these happy memories to himself. He would be seen sitting in his favorite reclining chair with a slight smile on his face, just staring into space. His wife knew what he was thinking about and had no interest in hearing about the farm life or country living.

One memory was a story told to Richard when he was a very young boy, by his grandmother. A tale about the crying woods.

Not far from where Richard grew up was a huge wooded area with a meandering creek curving through it. The creek had a supply of fish that was very tempting for a young boy and his favorite fishing pole on a sunny Saturday afternoon. And the woods were perfect for hunting with plenty of rabbit, squirrel, wild turkey, and even deer. Richard spent many happy hours as a youth in these woods. But he often felt as if someone or something was watching him. Sometimes he had the feeling of being followed, but he never heard footsteps or saw anyone.

There were times when he thought he heard crying, as if a woman were softly crying in the distance. He would hike and hike through the woods, walking very quietly and occasionally sitting on a fallen tree, looking and listening for the source of the crying. He never felt like he was getting any closer to the source of the crying, the sound was always just out of reach. The sound of the crying always remained a soft distant sound, a gentle sad crying. Richard, having many brothers and sisters, was sure that the crying was human and not the cry of a wounded animal.

Richard's grandmother would tell him about the Indian maiden and her sad story. Years and years before any of the white people came to settle in this area the Indians lived here. Some stayed for a long period of time and others just came to hunt, process the meat and the hides, and then would move on to other parts of the country after a few months.

As the white man moved westward from the east coast to settle the land, there were many conflicts with the Indians. The Native Americans did not want their hunting grounds destroyed by these foreign settlers. After many years of fighting, negotiations, more fighting, raids by both sides on each other, and more endless battles, sadly the Indians were forced from the area.

Near Richard's boyhood woods is an area where arrowheads were easily found nearly every spring when the ground was plowed for planting. The children loved walking the plowed fields and collecting the arrow heads. To them this was wonderful proof of the story that the Indians had lived in this gently rolling area for years and years. How exciting for young children to find the arrowheads!

The soil was excellent for growing corn and other crops. And the woods were probably a wonderful source of wild game, berries, and the creek provided plenty of fish. The family understood why the Indians lived in this area.

The tale is told of a young Indian boy on his first hunt with his father and a few other young Indian boys. As the group was slowly, very carefully following the trail of a large deer, no one spoke a single word and communication was only by hand signals or a slight nod of the head. The young boy's father was in the lead with the boys following carefully behind him doing their best to copy his every move and to prove that they could be great hunters.

Step by step they tracked the deer, watched and listened for an opportunity for the kill. The group came to a stop and quietly waited. No one moved. Even the breathing of the young boys was soft and quiet. Still the group remained on alert for the deer or any other useful game. Suddenly, a swoosh was heard and then a soft thump.

The father turned around to quiet the boys but was shocked to see the lifeless body of his young son lying on the ground with an arrow piercing his chest. The boy never cried out. With a loud piercing scream that could be heard throughout the woods, the father raced to the boy and cradled him in his arms. No one spoke a word.

Silently the group began the long walk back to camp. One young boy raced ahead to the camp to inform the others about the accident. In the woods the father gently picked up his son and carried him back to camp.

The boy's mother, crying and screaming raced out to meet them. Hours later as the body was being prepared for burial the mother became very quiet. She would sit on the ground and slowly rock back and forth, back and forth.

After a few days the mother would disappear for long stretches of time. Soon it was discovered that she had located the site where her son died. There she would sit in solitude for hours unable to stop crying. Time passed and the tribe decided it was necessary to move on to another area far away. After a few days of travel, the tribe discovered the mother was missing. A couple of the braves went back to the woods thinking that she would be there, visiting the site where her son died. As they came near to the location they heard a woman's crying and knew that they were right.

Slowly they walked through the trees barely making a sound. The braves did not want to be disrespectful of the grieving mother. But when they reached the location, the mother was there but sadly she was dead, and had been for several hours. The braves never did learn the source of the crying.

Richard's grandmother told him that he should never hunt for the crying source, that he should respect the Indian mother's grief and not disturb her. She taught Richard to always have respect for the dead.

To this day people who walk quietly in the woods will hear the soft, sad crying in the distance. Only the local residents who know the history understand the crying and do not search for the source.

Many years later after Richard and I became friends his health began to fail, and on a cold winter day he passed away quietly in his sleep at his home. His wife had him buried in a Dayton cemetery. Sadly, I had lost a good friend.

A few months later I was driving by my family's old farm in Darke County. Then on a whim I headed on down the road to where Richard grew up. My car radio was turned off and the windows rolled down as I drove slowly down the old country road, enjoying the sights and sounds of the country. Soon memories of Richard came to mind, how he loved the old family farm, and how he gave up his dreams for the woman he loved.

After driving further I came to the small, old cemetery where we both had distant relatives buried. I stopped to visit some of the graves and to walk through the old cemetery with the broken, faded markers and the fading names. Being in a quiet mood, I returned to my car and just sat there for a few minutes enjoying the quiet. Then I heard it. A deep male voice that softly said, “Thank you, thank you for sharing the old memories with me.”

I truly believe that the voice belonged to Richard and he finally came home to Darke County. His dream came true.

2. The Vanishing Man

Can big strong men become afraid of a ghost? Oh yeah, you bet they can. This story was shared with me a couple of years ago after one our yearly ghost walks in Greenville, Ohio.

David Winter was a young man in his mid 20's who bought his first house in New Madison, Ohio. It was a two story fixer upper but he did not care. It was his first house. It fit his budget and besides he enjoyed doing projects and rehabbing a house just had to be the ultimate project. It was a typical old small two story with two bedrooms and a bath upstairs and the kitchen and living room downstairs. Not a lot of room but it was all his and besides he could afford the payments. He was finally a home owner.

Now he could paint the walls any color he chose, hang pictures anywhere on the walls, it was his house and his choices. And his house would be a neat place for his buddies to hang out and watch football games on weekends or to enjoy a poker game.

A couple of his friends helped him to clean the place up. It was the usual old house clean up, clean some windows, paint a few walls, clean the bathroom, get a supply of food for the kitchen, and then move in the furniture. He was so eager to get moved in that he did not want to spend any more time than necessary on the cleaning. After all there was a football game on television in a few days and the cleaning could just wait!

Friday evening after the guys got off work they all loaded up their pickup trucks with Dave's furniture and his boxes of belongings and the moving began. The first priority was to get the TV in place and hook up the cable. After some TV time, the guys agreed to move the bedroom furniture upstairs along with some of the boxes of Dave's belongs.

Two of the men went outside to get the bed frame and the third fellow went upstairs to open the room doors and to turn on some lights. Suddenly he came racing downstairs. Not saying a word he quickly picked up a small piece of furniture and headed back upstairs close behind the other two men.

Sometimes the guys worked in pairs carrying the heavy items, but usually they worked alone carrying individual boxes upstairs. Finally everything was in the house and the guys went home leaving the new owner alone in his house. The owner thought that his buddies seemed to be in a big hurry to get to their own homes. But Dave guessed they were probably just tired.

Sunday soon arrived and the guys came over again to watch the afternoon football game. The owner asked if the guys wanted to go upstairs and see how he had arranged the furniture. Very quickly all three fellows simultaneously shook their heads no and said maybe some other time, quietly thinking to themselves that that time would be far, far in the future.

The guys enjoyed the game and afterwards they all decided to go out for a steak dinner. Finally the men started talking about the house and all the responsibilities involved in home ownership. Soon the age of the house became the topic and the guys wondered about the history of the old house.

The owner mentioned that he had no idea about the history of the house. All he knew was that the previous owner had died of old age and the house was sold by his daughter to settle the estate.

The guys all looked at each other and then the stories of their experiences began. One man mentioned how when he was alone upstairs on moving day he felt someone touch his arm, just a light tap on his shoulder as if to let him know someone else was there. He turned around to see who was there but saw no one. Another man told about feeling as if he was being watched but never seeing anyone or hearing any sounds.

The third man said that he when he went upstairs to turn on the bedroom lights he though he saw some mist in the room almost like a cloud of smoke but in the shape of a person. Then as he was coming down the stairs he had the scare of his life.

He had just started down the steps when he felt something brush quickly past him as if a person had walked by him and just lightly bumped him. He slightly turned his head to the right and saw the faint, misty figure of a man dressed in a suit and carrying a felt dress hat similar to the styles of the 1950s. The friend stopped moving and watched as the ghostly figure continued down the stairs and vanished straight through the front wall! Well, the friend very quickly ran down the rest of the stairs and out to the pickup trucks. For the rest of the evening he made sure that he was never alone on the stairs or anywhere upstairs.

During Dave's first night in the house he heard footsteps walking across the attic floor and then a door softly closing down the hallway from his bedroom. Dave carefully checked all though the attic and found no one else was in the house. The foot steps were too heavy to be an animal. Heading back to his bedroom Dave found the door to the second bedroom was shut and he was sure that he had left the door open. In fact, the door stop was still partially under the closed door.

The sound of conversations coming from the first floor is often heard during the night. When Dave first moved into the house he would carefully go downstairs to investigate the noise. The sofa cushions would have indentations in them as if someone were sitting down; the wood rocking chair would be slowly moving back and forth, and Dave would have the feeling that people were looking at him as if he just walked into a small party.

Dave told me that one evening he watched a show on television about ghosts and how residents of a house learned to live with them. So he decided to use their technique.

The next time he heard the voices during the night he walked downstairs to the living room and talked to the "house guests." Dave again did not see anyone there but he told the room that he would share the house with the "guests" if they would talk quietly and let Dave sleep peacefully at night. Now only on rare occasions will Dave hear the voices and that is always on the weekends when he does not need to get up early for work. They are learning to live together.

The owner said that a few days after moving into his house, a next door neighbor came over to welcome him to the neighborhood. During the course of their conversation, the neighbor asked Dave if he knew that his house was haunted. Dave said no and bravely started to laugh. When the neighbor stood quietly and did not laugh Dave became serious and said that would explain some of the sounds he hears.

The neighbor said that for years the house has been haunted but no harm ever came to anyone who lived in the house. According to the neighbor, the ghost was friendly. No one recalled any tragedy occurring in that house so the neighbors think it is just a previous owner who wants to stay there.

The new owner laughs about how his big strong buddies will not go upstairs because of the strange events. But the owner finds comfort in knowing that he is not alone in the house. After all this is Dave's house and he is willing to share his home.

Rita Arnold

3. The Disappearance

In reading the old newspapers I came across an interesting article of some strange happenings in Darke County. These events occurred around 1800, which was only a few years after the signing of the Treaty of Greenville.

The events took place over 200 years ago shortly after the turn of the century, in northern Mississinawa Township close to what is now referred to as North Dayton. At that time this area was thickly wooded with very few settlers whose homesteads were scattered about the area. There were dirt roads, and in many areas just narrow dirt paths, for travel which was accomplished by foot, on wagon, or on horseback.

When people would get together to help each other harvest the crops, or to visit, or to attend church, the children usually went off to play among themselves. The parents always told the children to stay where they could be seen and not to go play in the woods.

Children will be children and the woods were very tempting. After all, they were farm kids and thought they knew all about the woods. Hadn't their fathers taken the boys into the woods to hunt and the mothers taken the daughters into the woods to look for berries and flowers?

One year in the very early 1800's all the families decided to get together at the local church one Saturday for a day long picnic celebration. The church yard would be perfect for a huge picnic and plenty of room for the kids to play games. All the families were pleased with the recent harvest and everyone was ready for a day of fun and relaxation.

The food was set on make shift tables under some large shade trees. People filled their plates and began to sit on the ground in small groups to eat and talk. The children, being typical, ate quickly and went back to playing. Sometime during the afternoon the children began playing near the woods and even into the woods.

Around mid afternoon the families started to gather up all of their belongs to begin their journeys home. Being farm people they all had chores at home to attend to. The adults said their good-byes to each other and called for their children to come join them.

Soon the Harter's realized that young Sarah was missing. Thinking that she might be in the outhouse the mother sent her oldest daughter around back of the church to look for the girl. The girl returned but without Sarah. The Harter's checked with the other families and no one had seen Sarah for at least a couple of hours and maybe longer.

Now the family became very worried and all the families joined in the search for young Sarah. As night began to fall some of the men returned to their homes for lanterns, torches, and tracking dogs to aid in the search.

Eventually the searchers went into the forbidden woods. The children remained behind at the church with the women. The men went deeper and deeper into the dark woods. Occasionally they thought they saw movement in the distance, sometimes a searcher would be sure he heard footsteps, and one man swore he heard a child calling for daddy. But still Sarah remained missing.

After searching all that night and most of the next day, some of the men needed to return to their farms. The Harter's continued the search for several more days with the occasional assistance of their neighbors and then very sadly had to stop the search. Little Sarah was never found. No one is sure just what happened to her.

The family had a small private service for Sarah and placed a marker for her in the family cemetery. But they never felt satisfied. For the rest of their lives they had an empty feeling because they had no answers. No clues were ever found as to what happened to Sarah.

For many years after that tragic event at the yearly community picnic celebrating that year's harvest the people would report strange happenings in the woods. The thinking is, it was Sarah's ghost, or was it children playing tricks on other people?

Every year for years around harvest time the talk around the community was about the sad disappearance of Sarah.

Then shortly afterward the strange happenings in the woods would occur. People heard a child in the far distance faintly calling for help. But no one could find the source of the voice. And soon the howl of a wolf was heard. Sometimes the sound of someone running through the woods was heard but no one was found. And soon the howl of a wolf was heard.

Some people thought the howling of a wolf and ghostly sightings were connected. Some people felt that the causes of the 'ghostly happenings' were local children trying to scare other children.

In recent years I have not heard of any unusual sights or sounds from that woods, but who knows? Are we just not listening? Or are we not talking about what we see and hear?

Whatever happened to little Sarah?

Rita Arnold

4. Cemetery Happenings

One of the best locations for ghost sightings are cemeteries, especially the very old cemeteries or at least the oldest sections of cemeteries.

Darke County is very fortunate to have many old, special cemeteries. The Greenville Cemetery is special due to the one of a kind layout. The oldest sections have the small narrow roadways with just enough room for one car. In order for cars to pass each other they must drive partly on the grass. Then there are the tall mature, spreading trees that provide great shade on a sunny day.

And perhaps my favorite part is the fact that nothing, and I mean nothing, is in a straight line. If you want to read the tombstones of the graves you must walk in a zig-zag pattern and carefully watch your step because of the trees' roots and the uneven ground. Man, you just got to love old cemeteries!

This particular section contains many of the graves of the founders of Greenville and the surrounding area. Read the names on the tombstones and you are reading the history of the county. You are reading the names of the founding fathers, the movers and shakers from the very beginning of Darke County. How exciting to walk among history!

Not far from the Civil War monument is a large mausoleum which has been there for years. At least once a year someone will come up to me and tell me they have a story. The events always happen late in the evening as the sun is setting and the people are walking past the mausoleum.

So many people have talked about walking by this building and hearing muffled voices coming from inside the building. And this was with the door shut! Some say that it is just excellent imaginations but others say that the mausoleum is haunted.

Then there was the couple who was walking by and heard the door open and then foot steps on the front pavement.

Another time a couple was taking a walk with a small group of people in this section during the early evening hours. While listening to the speaker talk about Darke County history and the people buried in the Greenville cemetery, this couple who were standing at the back of the group, turned to look at the area behind them including where the mausoleum stood.

While still listening to the speaker the couple continued to study the mausoleum. Looking at the architecture and the aging exterior walls they noticed a man standing quietly in front of the building.

The couple turned back around to look at the speaker and to continue on with the walk. After a few minutes the lady asked her husband if he noticed the style of clothing on the stranger standing by the front of the mausoleum. They both started describing what they saw and agreed the dress style was from an earlier time period. Both people mentioned how the man was standing in front of the door as if he was waiting for the door to open.

After the walk had concluded the attendees thanked the speaker and everyone went their separate ways.

A few days later the couple was talking with others who had attended the walk and they all soon began describing the man in the old fashioned suit at the mausoleum. That's when a lady told the group the story of the man who haunts the building.

John was in his mid twenties and had lived in Greenville all his life. In fact John's family had moved to Greenville shortly before the Civil War. John was neither a famous business man, nor an elected city official. He was just an every day hard working man who worked at a general store. John did what ever was needed at the store, stocking the shelves, checking in orders, and waiting on customers.

Life was good for John. The only thing missing was a wife and John was sure that someday soon he would meet the woman of his dreams.

John's dream did come true the day he met Mary. Soon they were seen walking around town together, going to church socials, and occasionally enjoying a picnic along the Greenville Creek.

After a few months of dating, John popped the question and asked Mary to marry him. When she said yes John was the happiest man in the county.

The wedding date was set and the plans were made. John had bought a small house just a couple of blocks from the store. The house had a carriage house in back where he kept his horse and buggy.

Finally the wedding day arrived, a bright, sunny Sunday afternoon just perfect for a wedding at Mary's family home. John dressed in his best (and only) suit, and then went out back to hitch the horse to the buggy.

Mary waited with her family and friends at her home for John to arrive. The ceremony was to start at 1:30 but John was not there. At 2:00 Mary was in tears and worried about John and about what could have happened to him. Mary's father and brother told her that they would go look for the missing groom. The men were not sure if they should be concerned for his welfare or if they were mad at him for standing up Mary!

They decided to go to John's house and start there. After knocking on his door and not getting any answer they asked some of the neighbors if they had seen John. One of the neighbors suggested they look in the carriage house because he saw John headed that way earlier in the day and offered to go with the men. And there on the floor they found John.

John's horse was standing there with only part of his harness on; the reins were tangled around the horse's legs. There was blood on the right front hoof. John lay on the ground with a large head wound and blood splattered everywhere. John was dead.

It appeared that something had spooked John's horse causing the horse to rear and hit John in the head with a hoof. Now Mary's father had the unpleasant task of informing Mary about John's death.

John was quietly buried in the Greenville Cemetery under a large shade tree. After many years passed Mary did wed and lived a happy contented life in Greenville with her husband and children. Years later when Mary passed away she was buried in the mausoleum.

The Ghosts Among Us

People who have seen the ghostly figure of a man outside the mausoleum like to think that it is John coming to visit his beloved Mary.

Rita Arnold

Randolph County Stories

Rita Arnold

5. The Gangsters

Gangsters in Union City, Indiana? Bet I have your attention now!

Turn the clock back to the 1920's, the roaring 1920's. Remember the old movies about the gangsters, the movies with James Cagney, the Model A cars, the fast talking bad guys, and the rapid fire machine guns? Those are the visions I have when I think about the 1920s.

In the first half of the 1920's most travel of any distance was by train. Union City was a small but growing town with lots of train travel both passenger and freight trains. At that time Union City had the usual businesses, grocery stores, hardware store, grain elevator, feed mill, clothing shops, and a ladies hat store with a bar in the basement, and the usual miscellaneous stores. What? Back up! A bar? In the basement? Of a hat store?

A short distance north of the railroad tracks is the business district. One of the stores located on a corner has an outside access down to the basement. The old story is that there was an underground, 'secret' bar in the basement where 'certain' people traveling through the area would spend the evening hours. The bar would have people coming and going and plenty of noise so I am not sure just how much of a secret the bar was.

Times were different back then. If the 'visitors' wanted to come to Union City and spend some money, no one really cared as long as no crimes were committed.

The story as told to me is that when the gangsters from the larger cities, like Chicago, needed to "hide out" for awhile they would travel to small towns by train and stay for a few days and then move on to another town until they felt safe returning to their home town. People traveling by cars in those days were more noticed than train travelers since not many people owned a car. And the idea was to try to blend in with the locals. But with the gangster's fancy dress styles and the large amount of money they had to spend, they did not blend in very well.

One night when the bar was crowded, an argument broke out between two men. No one remembers what the fight was about. It just started between two men who had too much to drink.

It started with the exchange of words, than shouting, then pushing, and finally the bartender and a couple of bouncers told the men to take the disagreement outside. One thing lead to another, a gun was drawn and one man was fatally shot. The other gentleman took off running towards the tracks and hopped on a slow moving train, never to be seen again in Union City.

The local police were called to the scene but no one saw anything happen and in fact most people said that they did not hear anything. The majority of the local people did not want to get involved with these visitors or in any of their disagreements. The locals just wanted to be friendly and do a little business with the out of town visitors.

The man who was shot was buried quietly in the local cemetery just west of town. The names of the men involved are lost to history. Some of the residents would speculate that it was a big time gangster from Chicago. And the young children made a game out of imitating the shooting incident. The local authorities never located the shooter. The incident was generally forgotten as the years passed, and most of the local citizens from that time period either forgot about the event or just did not want to discuss it. Still some people enjoyed telling the story and with it's telling the gangster became more and more famous. And for years playing gangster was a favorite pastime of the young children.

Not many years after the shooting there were reports of a man walking rapidly down the street toward the tracks. He was dressed in a pin stripe suit, white dress shirt, with a wide tie, and a felt dress hat worn cocked on his head covering his right eye. He kept looking back over his shoulder and moving quickly toward the tracks.

While he was walking-running his right hand was always in his right jacket pocket. The pocket was bulging like he was holding an object.

The Ghosts Among Us

To this day occasionally late at night or very, very early in the morning a misty figure of a man is seen heading toward the tracks but looking back over his shoulder.

Many people speculate that the shooter is still running away from the bar.

Rita Arnold

6. The Man

If you leave Greenville, Ohio, and drive straight west, within a few miles you will come to the Indiana state line. There is not a town near this location. Not even a cluster of houses at the intersection of two roads. Just farm houses that dot the land spaced far apart with pastures and fields separating the farms.

This story takes place in a house that was built in the 1920's and had additions made over the years as different families lived in it. When you drive by this house there are really no outstanding features. Just a nice looking two story white wood framed home with lots of trees around the yard, and various shrubs that surround the house.

Rita Arnold

This is one of those small farms that had several owners throughout the years. Just everyday people trying to make a living by farming.

In the early 1940's the family that lived there had a son who was drafted and soon sent to Europe to fight in the war. Sadly one day the family received a telegram from the War Department telling them that their son had been killed in action.

This was a terrible blow to the husband who had planned to pass the farm on to his only son. The son's mother and sisters did their best to continue on with life. Everyone pitched in to help with the farm, hoping that with time the pain of losing a son and brother would ease.

The father did his best to continue. He worked the farm as best as he could, but his heart and soul were not in it. Sadly one day a daughter found him hanging in a corner of the barn from a wooden rafter.

To this day livestock will become spooked if stabled in this corner. People who are working in the barn will sometimes feel a strange sensation when in this corner, like a sadness. They will find themselves speaking softly to each other as if they were at a funeral or in church.

Occasionally it has been reported that someone will hear the sound of a rafter groaning as if a heavy object is swinging from a rope tied to it.

No one has reported seeing anything unusual. Just a felling of sadness and the sound of a rafter creaking and groaning.

Rita Arnold

7. The Cemetery

Northwest of Union City is a small old fashioned church painted white located just off a highway along a country road. The church is next to a large cemetery. In fact the oldest part of the cemetery is located across the street.

Being located outside of town, there is not much traffic going past to disturb anyone. If no one else is visiting the cemetery the only sounds are the squirrels running around and the birds singing their songs.

In fact I am very familiar with this cemetery because I have relatives buried there. I love the location of this cemetery. I have always considered this the perfect cemetery because of the location and the beauty. The quiet surroundings are very peaceful with plenty of shade from the large old trees.

Many of the graves in the oldest section are dated from the 1800's. As you read the tombstones you discover the names of some of the early settlers who helped develop this area.

Living over thirty minutes away from this cemetery I have only visited during the daytime hours. The events that occur here have not been witnessed during the daytime.

The story told to me is that at night hovering over some of the graves is seen a misty presence in a human form. The forms will move around the cemetery just above the ground but never leave the cemetery. The forms do not walk but just slowly float. The mist will rise up from various graves on various nights and be seen floating slowly about.

No one knows of any tragic accidents that have happened here or why this happens.

I want to think kindly about these events, believing that these misty forms represent former residents who are still visiting like neighbors do. And maybe keeping watch over the cemetery and the surrounding area for any changes.

Rita Arnold

Preble County Stories

8. The Eaton Store

South of Greenville, Ohio is pretty Preble County. This is your typical farming country with gently rolling fields and country roads curving around the farms. Doting the landscape are cloisters of homes and the scattering of small, pretty towns. This is one of the counties that you just enjoy driving through and spending time viewing the scenic countryside and meeting the people. You can travel south on one of the main highways and find yourself in the town of Eaton, Ohio.

Most of this area still has evidence that Indians resided here long before the arrival of the white man. There are trees with branches formed as markers for locating trails or a stream with fish.

Rita Arnold

Back then the area was thick with woods and various wild animals. The Native Americans were living here supporting their families without destroying the land.

As our country started to develop, the population began to move west for adventure and for the homestead opportunities. There were only a few major dirt trails wide enough for wagon trains that lead to the western lands. One major trail is now known as Route 40. Along this route thousands and thousands of people headed west by wagon train and horse back. When some of the adventurers reached what was to become western Ohio they headed south of the trail to settle and build their homesteads in what is now called Preble County.

Soon the town of Eaton developed and became the main place to open a business be it retail or professional, and a great place to live.

As time passed the fact that this was originally Indian land was soon forgotten and the growth and development of new businesses became one of the main focuses of the town.

The Ghosts Among Us

There was a vacant piece of land just north of the town located on one of the main roads. This plot was not farmed for as long as anyone could remember. It was just weeds, wildflowers, and plenty of trees. No one knows why but the land was never worked, it just set idle.

One day an out of town developer saw the land and decided that would be a great location to build a large retail department store. The big earth moving equipment was brought in to clear the trees and level the land and soon the building was completed along with a large paved parking lot.

The store was filled with a huge variety of goods and the people came from all over the area to shop. Employees of all ages were hired to work in the store, everyone from high school age to the retired person looking for some part time work.

The store was open long hours every day including holidays. Employees were always coming and going at various times and their work was spread out throughout the entire store including working in the store offices.

It was not long before the employees realized that no one wanted to be alone in certain locations of the store. When the employees began to share their stories they found that they all had similar experiences.

Can a shoe department be dangerous? Well, maybe not dangerous but strange events can and do happen.

It has been reported by different people that when stocking inventory in the shoe department one must be careful, be very careful. You see, if you are alone in the shoe department occasionally shoes will fly off the shelf. Not the box, not the pair, just one shoe at a time will be lifted out of the box. Usually this will happen when the shoes are not placed neatly and in the proper place. The employees said that as they move down the aisle stocking the shelves they will see the shoes flying off the shelves – one shoe at a time. The shoes will not just fall off the shelf but will fly across the aisle and land with a loud thud on the floor!

The office personnel have reported the office chairs will suddenly roll quickly across the floor when no one is close to the chair. Not just a gentle roll but a strong fast rolling movement that ends with a bang against the wall. This only occurred when just one person was in the room. It is as if someone gave the chair a push and off it went. At first the office people were scared and they would quickly leave the room. Now the employees accept this chair movement as part of working in the office.

The employees have a lounge where they can enjoy an occasional break, drink some coffee, and just sit and relax for a few minutes. This is a room where you do not want to be alone. When by yourself, there are times when the room is so quiet that you can just barely hear a soft humming. Almost like a chant with a steady rhythm. The employees have found themselves humming this beat when they return to work. No one has found the source of the humming.

Then there are the occasional times when employees feel like someone is watching them but no one is around, neither customers nor co-workers. They do not feel like they are in danger, but they know someone is carefully watching.

What could be causing all these events to happen?

Research has found that this area was probably an Indian burial ground. No bones were reportedly found when the store was being built but who knows – was something found in the ground? Maybe some land is just not meant to be developed.

9. The Lewisburg Library

Have you ever been to the library in Lewisburg, Ohio?

Well one day I received an email inviting me to visit the library because a couple of employees wanted to talk with me. They asked if I would like to hear about their resident ghost. Of course, I said yes and soon I was on my way to Lewisburg. There I spent a pleasant evening with two very wonderful, interesting people.

The library is located on the main street in center of town. The building was donated to the town by Anna Brown.

In the early 1900's Anna Brown and her father lived in Lewisburg where he was the only town physician. He was able to provide a very good living for his family.

Anna, his daughter, who never married, died as young lady in the early 1930's. Anna lived with her father her entire life.

When I read Anna's last will and testament she listed dispositions donating large sums of money to her church and to various friends, large sums of money to Miami Valley Hospital, to St. Elizabeth Hospital, to Good Samaritan Hospital, to Stillwater Sanatorium of Montgomery and Preble Counties for the specific treatment of Tuberculosis, a Franklin car to a friend, Haviland china and silverware to a friend, a large diamond ring to a friend, money to maintain the Brown cemetery lot, and the home property to the Village of Lewisburg for use as a public library and "which building should be known as The Brown Library."

With the monetary donation to the hospitals for the treatment of Tuberculosis I wonder if Anna died from that terrible disease.

Anna had a love of books and wanted others in town to find pleasure in reading just as she had. By donating her home she knew that her beautiful house would not go to ruin and it would help the town to afford a library for the town's people.

Not only did she donate her house but also all the books that she owned which was a large collection of reading material. In May, 1935, the deed was transferred and filed in the Probate Court of Preble County and The Brown Library was established.

The first floor holds the large collection of books. It is easy to tell the original part of the house from the sizable addition that has been added onto the back of the building. The new addition is nice and roomy with plenty of chairs.

But the older rooms are my favorite. The high ceiling, the old windows, the wood floors that will creak when people walk on them, and the beautiful wood stairway leading up to the second floor are all part of the attraction of the older rooms. And here you will find Anna.

Yes, Anna has been reported as still being seen in her beloved home.

Go up the old wood stairs and you will find a room that is now used for meetings. Here the employees will notice the strong smell of roses. In the center is a large rectangular wood table surrounded by chairs. Along one wall are built in old wood cabinets used for storage. The cabinet doors are never left open. They are always shut with a strong latch. The employees will sometimes enter the room only to find the cabinet doors standing wide open. They can only open if the latch was turned.

There are employees who will smell the aroma of fresh baked cookies when entering a room. Some have reported lights being turned on when no one is near the light switch.

There are times when books fall off the shelves. Not just fall, but will fly off the shelves and land across the aisle. Too far for a book to just fall off the shelf by itself. This will happen when no one is near that section of the shelf.

Employees have reported that at times when they enter a room they feel a definite chill. Not a breeze or a draft but a cold spot. This does not happen all the time and not always at the same time or the same day.

One employee entered the children's book area and saw the figure of a woman sitting in a rocker. She was dressed in a style from years ago, with a bow in her hair. The employee just stood there looking at the woman not recognizing who she was. Then the employee suddenly remembered that no one had entered the children's area for quite a while. After one or two minutes the figure just vanished and the rocker stood empty.

Another time before the library opened, an employee was preparing for the day. She knew that the doors were still locked and no one else was around. Suddenly she heard a swish. Like the sound that a long flowing skirt would make when a lady is walking. The employee said "Good morning Miss Brown."

A former employee requested and was granted permission to spend the night alone in the library, and she said that she heard voices inside the library but no one else was with her. It was as if people were having a pleasant conversation.

When the cleaning people are in the building after closing time they have seen shadows. After investigating they have found that no else but the cleaning crew are there. They did not hear voices or see anyone, only the shadows.

For holidays the employees will decorate the library rooms. There are times when decorations will be hung from the ceilings using hooks or maybe fishing line. Apparently Miss Brown does not always like the decorations because sometimes in the morning the employees will find the decorations on the floor. It will look as if the decorations were carefully laid on the floor. The hooks and fishing line were still secure in the ceiling. There was no way the decorations could have fallen from the ceiling.

A heavy tarp was used to cover one of the free standing shelves. The books were left in place because the workers knew that the tarp was adequate protection. At the end of the day the tarp remained over the books and everyone left the building locking the doors. The next morning the first two people entered the building together and found one of the books on the floor four or five feet away from the shelf.

On the first floor is a beautiful large picture of Miss Brown. Looking at the picture you have the feeling she is looking proudly at her home and the people now enjoying it as a library. One morning after some items had been moved around the day before, Miss Brown's picture was found placed on the floor facing the wall! The frame and glass were not broken or damaged. It was as if the frame was placed gently on the floor. The employees think that she was unhappy with the rearrangement of some of the items.

Everyone seems to enjoy telling about their experiences with Miss Brown. No one in the library has ever been harmed or felt threatened while in the building. They just have the feeling that she does not want to leave her home and is enjoying the library.

The old cemetery containing the Brown family plot is located very near the library. It's just a small cemetery with old faded tombstones marking the graves of some of the town residents from years ago.

Anna had her tombstone prepared before she died and she left money for the Brown family plot to be maintained. So where is the grave?

Many people have searched the cemetery using various maps and different techniques but no can find Anna's grave.

Is that why Anna remains in her house?

10. The Country Road

Like all rural counties Preble County has its share of winding, hilly, narrow roads. Most of these roads started out as dirt roadways for the farm wagons to travel.

Years ago in the 1800's the farm houses were located far apart with fields of crops and pastures in between. A large part of the county was still thickly wooded with old mature trees and plenty of wild game.

People could travel for many miles without seeing anyone. Farmers would hitch their horses to their wagons and travel to a field and begin working. Often they would take their lunch with them and then return home at the end of the long hard day.

Rita Arnold

This was a time before the cell phone, the walkie-talkies, or any other form of electronic communication. If an accident happened, you just had to wait until someone came along who could help or go for the help you needed.

There is a seldom used county road in the western part of Preble County that has an interesting story. The few people who live along this road will tell you about the unusual sounds they heard throughout the day.

The residents have told me that if they are walking along the road during the quiet of the evening they hear the sound of an old wooden wagon with horses hitched to it. Occasionally the soft voice of a driver urging on the team can be heard. No one has seen anything at these times, they just hear the sounds of a horse and wagon moving along the road.

During the mid 1800's a man was driving his team out to the fields one morning when something suddenly spooked his horses causing them to run out of control. The wagon hit a hole in the road then over turned throwing the driver off the wagon. He hit the ground hard breaking his neck.

That evening when the farmer did not return home from the fields his family went looking for him. Soon he was found lying dead in the roadway. The farmer was buried in the family plot on the farm. That land is still being farmed.

Over the years the name of the family has been forgotten but the sad tale of the driver dying continues to be handed down from generation to generation.

With the wagon sound only heard in the evening hours people wonder if the driver is trying to return to his family.

Rita Arnold

11.The West Manchester House

I was at a book signing where an older lady came up to me and wanted to tell me about her old house.

She lives in one of the oldest houses in town and has for over 40 years. She raised four children in that house. Her husband died many years ago of heart disease. The only thing she knows about the house is that the couple who sold the house to her had lived there for over 50 years.

All the years that she has lived in that house she has experienced certain events that she did not share with her family, just her close friend.

She told about the lights turning on with no one in the room, a rocking chair that rocked with no one sitting in it.

Then one day she saw the newspaper which was left on the couch float through the air and land on the coffee table. It was as if someone lifted the newspaper and gently laid the paper on the table.

She told me that every night she cleans the kitchen and makes sure that all the dishes are put away. Nothing is left on the counter top. Occasionally in the morning she will find a dirty coffee cup and saucer on the counter (she lives alone and always uses a coffee mug never a cup and saucer). Sometime she feels as if something is watching her when she is cleaning the house. But for some reason she never feels threatened or scared.

She told me that all of her children have their own families and live out of town but she still lives alone in the old house.

She does not want to tell her children for fear they may think she is getting old and crazy.

I made note of what she told me and thanked her for buying my books. Other people came and went as the afternoon wore on.

Near the end of the afternoon a lady in her twenties rushed into the store. She came right over to my table and bought my books. She said she just drove into town and was on her way to visit her mother. She then began to tell me about the house where she grew up in West Manchester. This lady related the same episodes!

She then told me that she wanted to buy my books for her mother as a gift. The younger lady was debating about telling her mother the stories of the strange events in the house. She was afraid that her mother would think she was crazy.

I advised her to tell her mother and said that I thought her mother would understand.

Rita Arnold

In closing -

You've scanned all the words,
You've read all of the pages,
You've learned to love the ghosts,
Who have been with us for ages!

Now it's time to give some thought,
To things that might be scary,
In order to be a real live ghost,
You've got to be at the cemetery!

Milton Arnold

www.ingramcontent.com/pod-product-compliance
Lightning Source LLC
LaVergne TN
LVHW050938080826
845145LV00004B/1319

* 9 7 8 0 9 7 8 8 4 6 3 9 8 *